A Job for Lightning

𝒟ISNEY PRESS
New York • Los Angeles

© Disney•Pixar

Everyone has a job
in Radiator Springs.
What can Lightning do?

© Disney•Pixar

Can Lightning water flowers?
No. Red can.

Can Lightning stack tires?
No. Guido can.

Can Lightning carry cars?
No. Mack can.

Can Lightning tow cars?
No. Mater can.

Can Lightning paint?
No. Ramone can.

Can Lightning race?
Yes, he can.
Ka-chow!